This book belongs to

Beeatrice

How the World

Learnt your Name

Paddy Morton

illustrated by
Georgina Moir

"Have **you** heard?"
"Well did you **know**?"

There's a story to treasure as you grow...
That long ago the friendly bees were sworn
To tell the world when you were born.

When that day came, and the sun raised its head,
Old Albert the beekeeper ran out and said

"Awake sleepy bees and listen well
there's a new baby come, we've the world to tell!"

Well I'll tell you,
that caused a stir!
the most excited,
were Beeatrice and Fleur.

"A new baby – bless me,
what great news
Come on, stop playing,
there's no time to lose."

"So open the doors and out we all go...
Where first? The trees or the flowers we know?"

Well some buzzed south...
...and some wiggled west
Some zoomed to the birds singing in their nest.

Straight across
the garden the
happy friends flew,
to tell the daisies waking in the dew...

"Wake up!"

"Wake up
you sleepy heads!
and tell the world what Albert said."

Other bees a different route they took,
to the great old oak beside the brook,
But old was he and hard of hearing,
"Shout louder bees, raise your cheering!"

Nearby in a glade the woodland creatures met,
The deer, the mole and the badger from his set,
Hedgehogs and hares, foxes and mice,

"Is that your name? That's ever so nice!"

And so your name travelled far and wide
Across field... pond... lake and mountainside.
The wind took it up and blew it to the sea.
Where whales spread the news,
(a bit wet for the bee!)

And now all the world has heard your name,
All plants, animals, birds, wild and tame,

And they all say

"Glad you're here how do you do?"
"Can't wait to meet you,
come and see us won't you?"

So as you get bigger you can be sure of one thing
that all the world joins in the happiness you bring
and as your life carries with it - events big and small
Don't forget, the world cares, so ...

"Tell the Bees" them all!

Where did this story come from?

The story of "How the world learnt your name"
is based on the old British tradition of "telling the bees".
Not so long ago bees and the beekeeper were a
central part of every community providing a
vital resource – HONEY! (Yum).

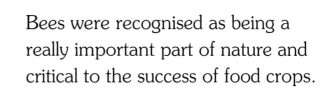

Bees were recognised as being a
really important part of nature and
critical to the success of food crops.

It was also noted how they came into contact
with all the plants and animals during their busy
day – they were everyone's friend!

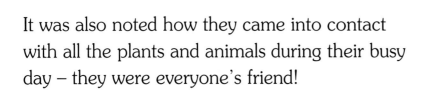

As we are all part of nature, the environment and the world it became a tradition to "Tell the bees" as soon as possible after a new baby was born into a community and often in fact any important news!

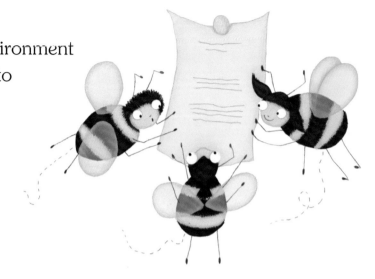

Someone had to spread the news when we arrived, and who better than the friendly bees.

So don't forget whenever you have a new member of the family or other important news, let the world know! - TELL THE BEES!

You can tell the bees your news at www.tellthebees.co.uk